MW00862391

Eric Marienthal's
COMPREHENSIVE JAZZ
STUDIES & EXERCISES
for all instruments

Editor: Larry Clark
Art Design: Odalis Soto
Photography: Karen Miller
Production Coordinator: Edmond Randle

TABLE OF CONTENTS

CHAPTER 1. "MAJOR CHORD SCALE EXERCISES"

Part 1. Scales and Exercises 6

Part 2. Motif Exercises 13

Part 3. "Finger Busters" 24

Part 4. Extended Motifs 26

Part 5. Ideas for Improvising 30

CHAPTER 2. "MINOR CHORD SCALE EXERCISES"

Part 1. Scales and Exercises 36

Part 2: Motif Exercises 45

Part 3. "Finger Busters" 56

Part 4. Extended Motifs 58

Part 5 Ideas for Improvising 63

CHAPTER 3. "UNALTERED DOMINANT CHORD SCALE EXERCISES"

Part 1. Scales and Exercises 68

Part 2: Motif Exercises 75

Part 3. "Finger Busters" 84

Part 4. Extended Motifs 86

Part 5 Ideas for Improvising 91

CHAPTER 4. "MELODIC MINOR SCALE EXERCISES"

Part 1. Scales and Exercise 97

Part 2: Motif Exercises 107

Part 3. "Finger Busters" 117

Part 4. Extended Motifs 120

Part 5 Ideas for Improvising 126

CHAPTER 5. "DIMINISHED CHORD SCALE EXERCISES"

Part 1. Scales and Exercises 131

Part 2: Motif Exercises 137

Part 3. "Finger Busters" 147

Part 4. Extended Motifs 149

Part 5 Ideas for Improvising 154

CHAPTER 6. "PENTATONIC AND BLUES SCALE EXERCISES"

Part 1. Scales and Exercises 158

Part 2: Motif Exercises 172

Part 3. "Finger Busters" 182

Part 4. Extended Motifs 184

Part 5 Ideas for Improvising 189

Introduction

The inspiration for writing this book was to create a series of technique building exercises as well as some useful melodic and harmonic studies and incorporate them into one format. Setting up a daily practice routine is vital to becoming a more proficient player. This book uses various scales and melodic motifs to explore ways of approaching different chord types. The idea is to study these scales and exercises in a way that will be useful for improvisation while, at the same time, providing a practice routing that simply helps improve your technique.

This book is based on the six chord scales most commonly used in improvising, no matter what style of music. They are:
1. The Major Chord Scale
2. The Minor Chord Scale (specifically Dorian Minor)
3. The Dominant Chord Scale (The Mixolydian Mode)
4. The Melodic Minor Scale
5. The Diminished Scale
6. The Pentatonic and Blues Scales

Each chapter is dedicated to a different scale and is divided into five parts:

PART ONE: "CHORD SCALE EXERCISES"

Part One introduces the chord scale of each chapter. Each key has its scale and corresponding exercise and each exercise has a different melodic and rhythmic treatment. It's important to learn each scale and working on them in this way creates a more interesting and useful practice routine.

PART TWO: "MOTIF EXERCISES"

This is an exercise that starts with a single short melodic idea. The idea, or motif, is first played in half-steps both ascending and descending. With each successive exercise the interval between motifs grows wider by half-steps until the interval between motifs reaches an octave. Even though the motif stays the same, as the interval widens, each exercise presents a new technical challenge.

PART THREE: "FINGER BUSTERS"

The idea behind this set of exercises is to help build strong technique and endurance, just as the name implies. Each "FINGER BUSTER" corresponds with the chord type of its chapter. The most benefit will come if each exercise is repeated at least four times. Try to build up to the point where you can make it to the end of number 50 with as few breaks as possible. You can almost think of this as the "workout" portion of each chapter and if you stay with it, you should really notice the benefit.

PART FOUR: "EXTENDED MOTIFS"

One valuable way to practice is to take a melodic phrase and practice in every key. Part Four uses this idea and is based on five different phrases written chromatically. Each phrase is derived from the chord type emphasized in that chapter. As the phrase changes key, keep the key of the chord in mind as well. Some of these exercises tend to be quite long in order to cover as much of an instrument's range as possible so feel free to break them up to make them easier to finish.

PART FIVE: "IDEAS FOR IMPROVISATION"

This final section of each chapter deals with a solo that was written to show different ways to use the chord scales over various sets of chord changes. As you play through each solo you'll see phrases pointed out to show how they relate to the chords and how various scales are used. I'm sure that, as you play through them, you'll find many more ways to use these chord scales and melodic ideas.

Tips on How To Use This Book

1. Try to always use a metronome to practice with. As I said before, this is as much of an exercise book as it is a harmonic studies book. The metronome is an important technique building tool because it guides you and makes sure that all your notes are being played evenly. Make sure that you can hear it as loudly as you can hear yourself and keep each note right in time. As you practice, set the metronome at different tempos and never play an exercise faster than you can control. The best way to become faster on your instrument is to first practice slowly and be very definite with each note.

2. Before you sit down to practice, decide which exercises you want to work on and set a goal for yourself. For example, practice parts One, Two and Three of a chapter one day and Four and Five the next. Or take certain lines out of each chapter and create your own routine. However it's put together, if you set a goal for yourself before you start, you'll probably be more likely to stick with it and really maximize your practicing time.

3. This book was written as a way of showing how you can use melodic ideas to become more familiar with certain chords and chord scales while building technique at the same time. But it's just the beginning! The optimum way to use this book is to work on the written exercises first and then challenge yourself by coming up with some of your own ideas and motifs and practice them in the same format. By practicing ideas off the top of your head, you'll be exercising your brain as well as your fingers!

Notes

This book was designed to fit the range of most instruments. Since certain instruments don't have a range lower than low B or higher than high F♯, optional notes are provided so that all of the exercises can be played on just about any instrument. These optional notes are written in parentheses and hopefully don't create too much of a distraction.

Also, during all the time I spent working on this book I struggled with the question of "courtesy accidentals" and whether or not to use them. It's important to practice remembering accidentals written early in a measure so that you don't forget to use them on the same notes later in the measure. But, at the same time, concentrating on playing an exercise correctly can be hard enough without having to think about remembering accidentals in measures that are more complicated. I suppose that the bottom line is to just keep your eyes open!

I'd like to thank Chick Corea, Michael Brecker, John Patitucci, Frank Gambale, Pat Kelley and Eddie Daniels for their valuable advice during the writing of this book.

CHAPTER ONE
MAJOR CHORD SCALE EXERCISES

Part One: Scales and Exercises

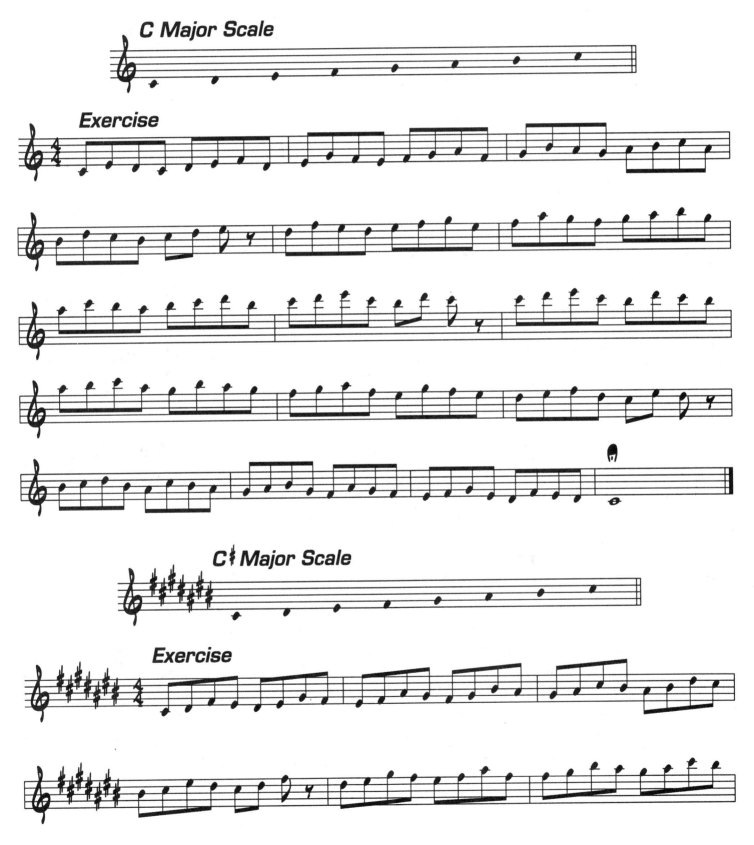

D Major Scale

Exercise

E♭ Major Scale

Exercise

E Major Scale

Exercise

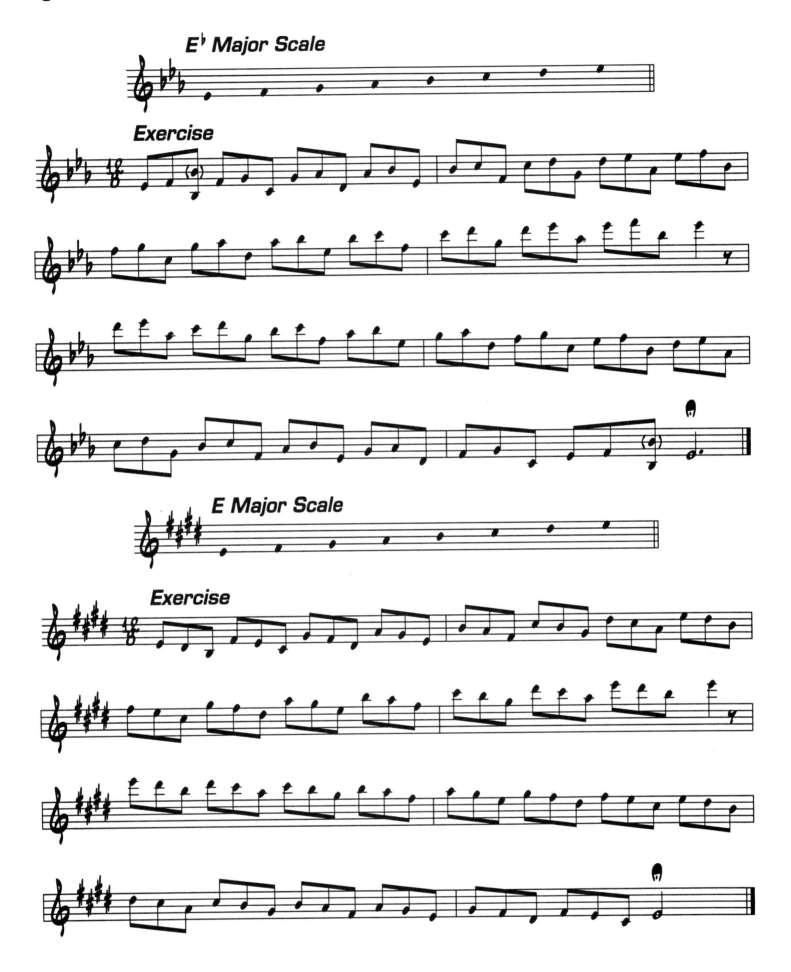

F Major Scale

Exercise

F♯ Major Scale

Exercise

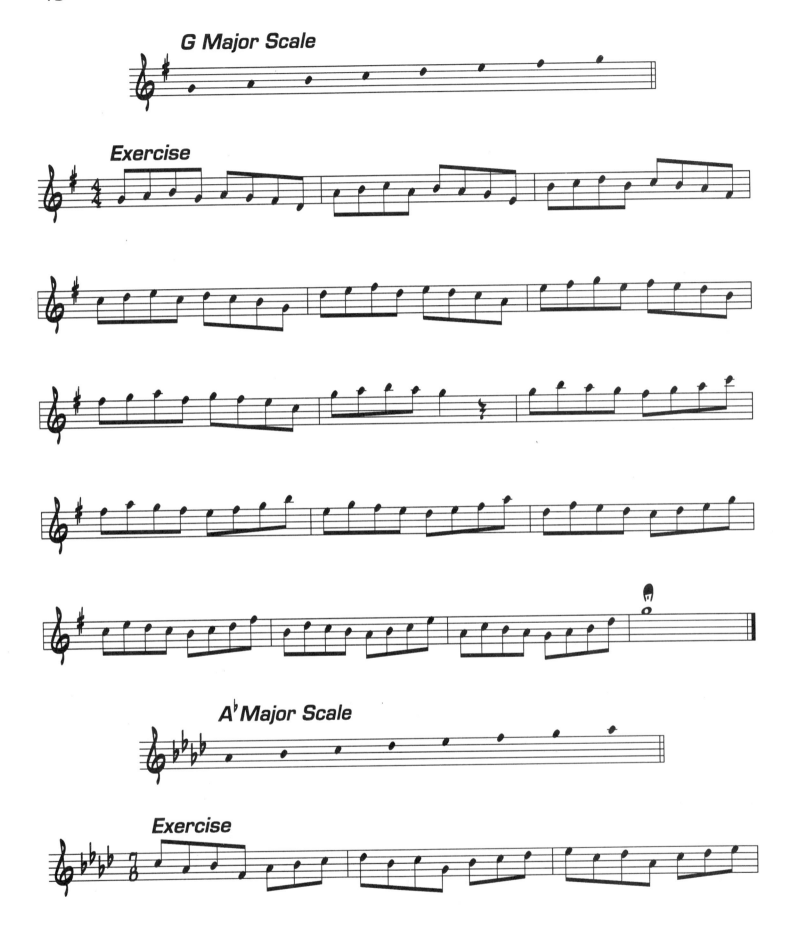

G Major Scale

Exercise

A♭ Major Scale

Exercise

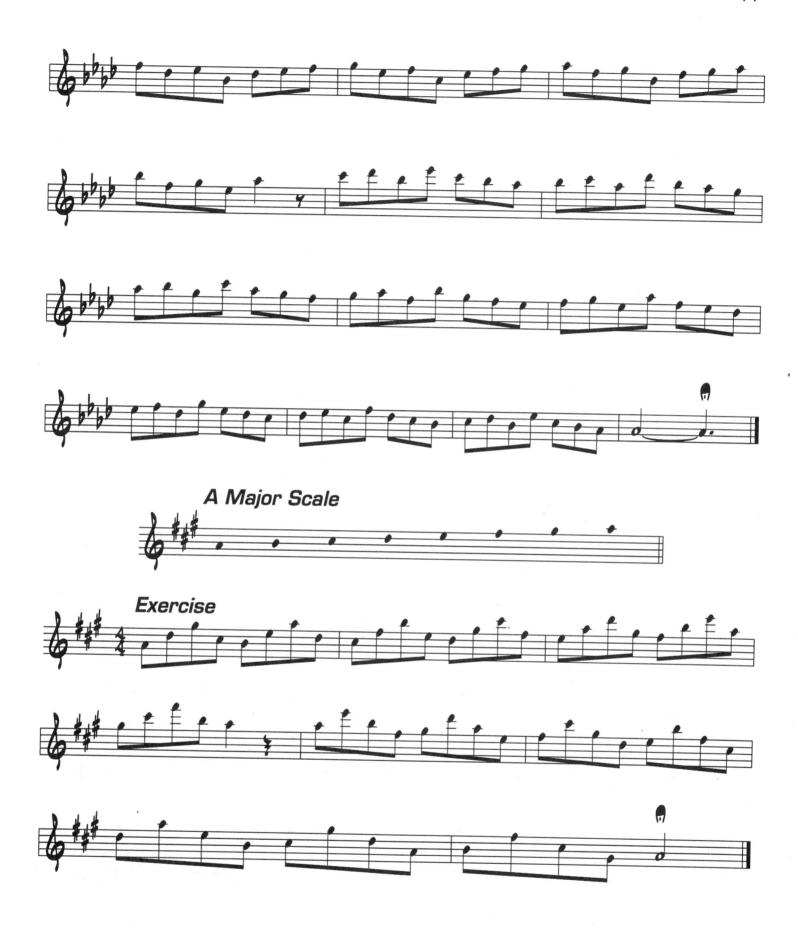

A Major Scale

Exercise

12

B♭ Major Scale

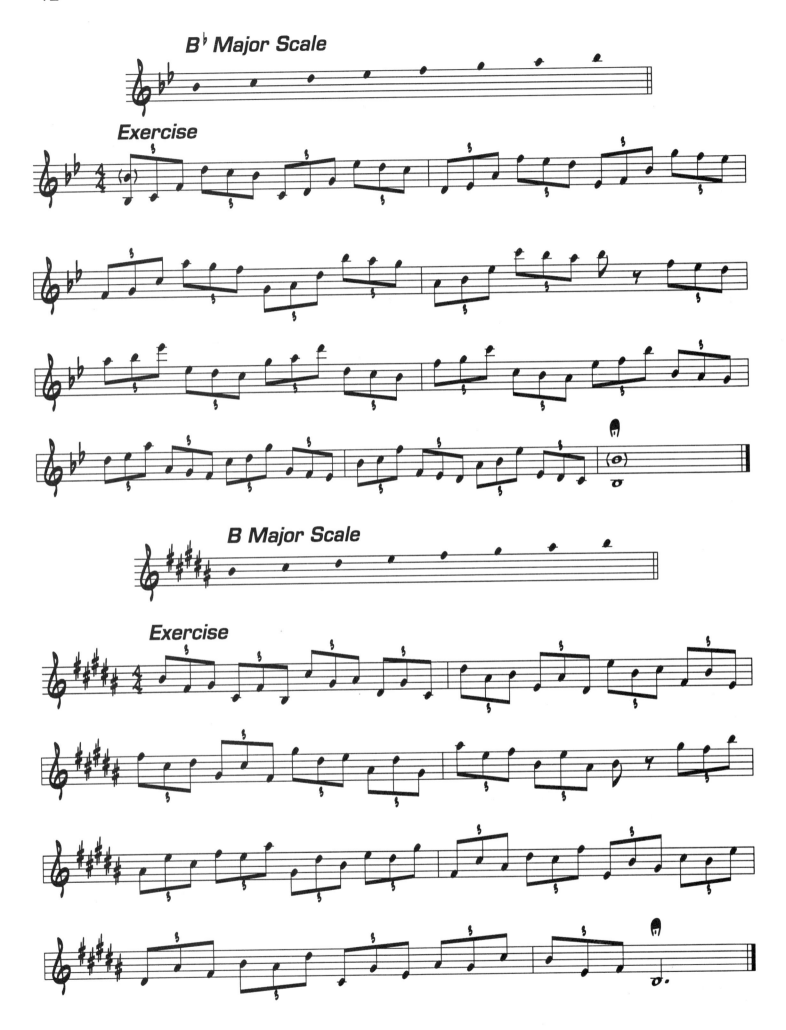

Exercise

B Major Scale

Exercise

13

Part Two: Motif Exercises

1

Minor 2nd's

EL96113

14

2

Minor 2nd's

Major 2nd's

Minor 3rd's

Major 3rd's

18

Perfect 4th's

Tri-Tones

Perfect 5th's

Minor 6th's

Major 6th's

Minor 7th's

Major 7th's

Octaves

3

Minor 2nd's

Major 2nd's

Minor 3rd's

22

Major 3rd's

Perfect 4th's

Tri-Tones

Perfect 5th's

Minor 6th's

Major 6th's

Minor 7th's

Major 7th's

Octaves

Part Three: "Finger Busters"

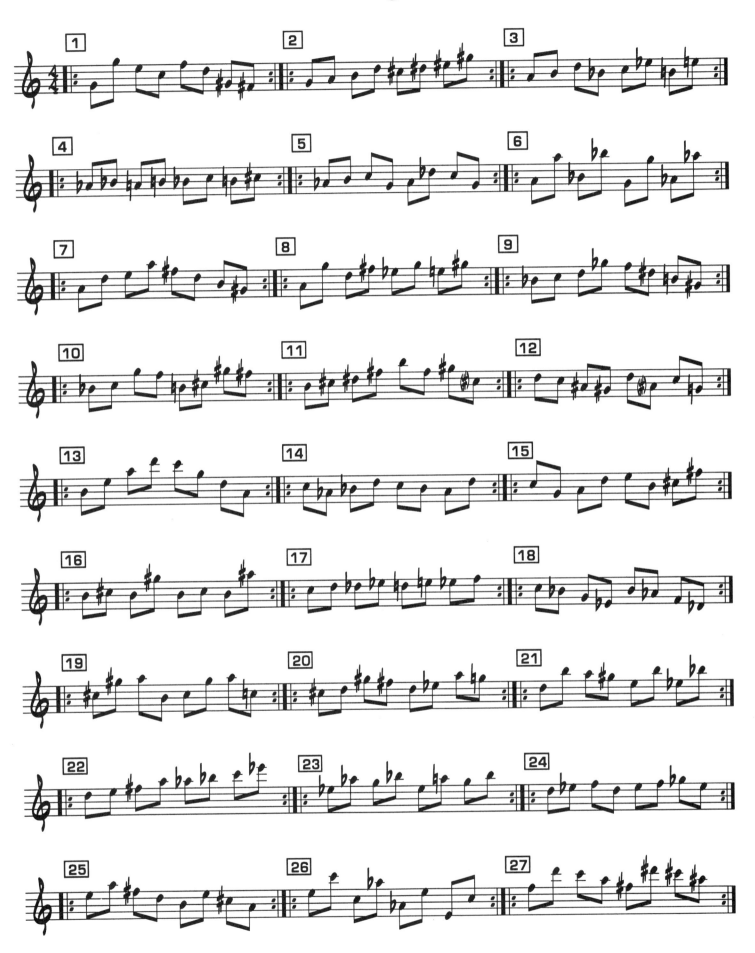

Part Four: Extended Motifs

Part Five: Ideas for Improvising

This section deals with a solo written over the tune, "Confirmation". Because this tune involves Major chords, a lot of the ideas in this chapter can be applied. As you play through this solo, try to see how each phrase fits into the chord above. The strong parts of the chord (root, 3rd, and 5th) are used as pivot points and the scale tones and chromatic passing tones are used to help shape the phrases.

#1. This is a good example of a phrase that emphasizes the stong parts of each chord and uses scale and passing tones to create a melody.

#2. This is one of many 2-5-1 progressions in this tune. As you can see by the chart below, the II and the V chords are related or "Diatonic" to the I chord. All the notes of any scale are refered to as being diatonic to that scale. If you use a C Major scale, for example, and build on each degree of that scale, you can see how the diatonic chords are formed:

Ex.1
Diatonic Chord Chart

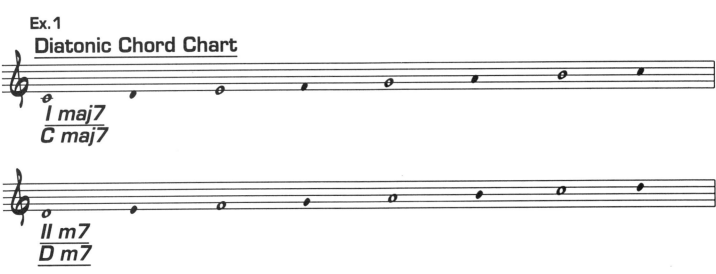

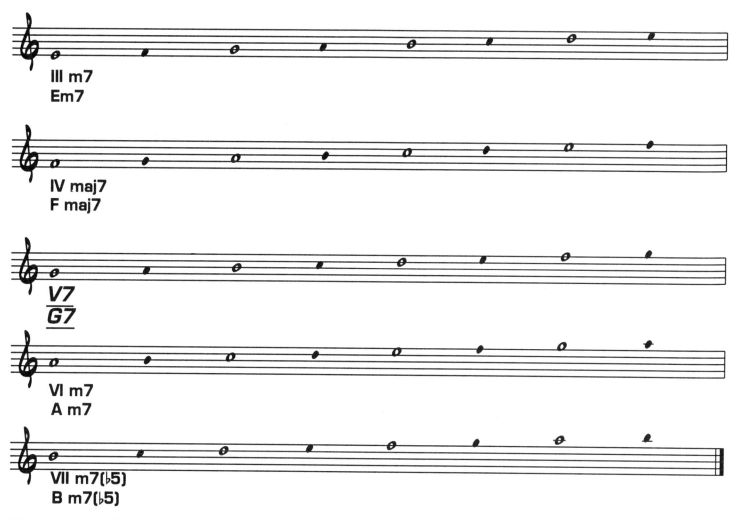

III m7
Em7

IV maj7
F maj7

V7
G7

VI m7
A m7

VII m7(♭5)
B m7(♭5)

The root, 3rd, 5th, and 7th of each chord tells you what type of chord it is. As you can see in this case, the "II", "V", and "I" chords become Dm7, G7, and CMaj7. Of course, there are many different types of II-V-I's. This is only one example and as you can see, this tune is based on II-V-I's.

#3. Most types of chords include notes that do not appear in the basic chord scale but sound good and add a different color or characteristic to your melody. These notes are called "tensions". Here are the available tensions for Major chords:

Ex.2
C Major

9th   ♯11th   13th

Available "Tensions"

Take another look at the diatonic chord chart. Each of the scales are diatonic to the key of "C". Each of these seven scales are called "Modes". Here is the same chart with the names of each mode:

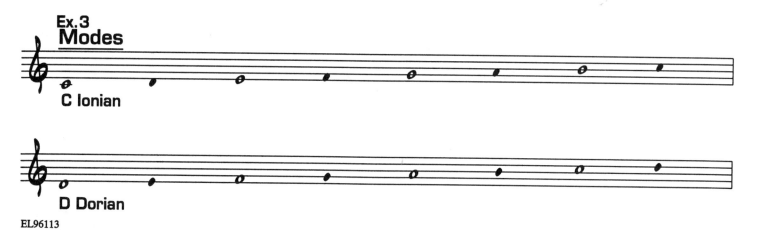

Ex.3
Modes

C Ionian

D Dorian

EL96113

E Phrygian

F Lydian

G Mixolydian

A Aeolian

B Locrian

An F Maj7 chord with the tension (#4) or (#11) would be called F Maj7(#11) and would use an F Lydian scale as its chord scale. Here are some melodic examples:

Ex.4

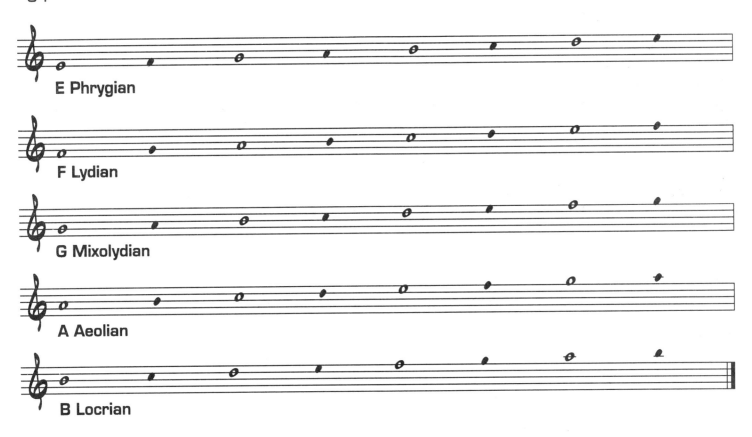

F maj 7(#11)

Ex.5

G maj 7 (#11)

Ex.6

Quick Reference

CHORD SCALE: Major   Maj.(♯11) or Lydian

CHORD TYPE:

Major	Maj.(♯11) or Lydian
Maj. Triad	Maj. 7th(♯11)
Maj. 6th	Maj. 13th(♯11)
Maj. 7th	
Maj. 9th	
Maj. 6/9	
Maj. 13th	
*min. 7th(♯5)	

*You can use the Major scale a minor 3rd above the root of the chord. Cm7(♯5), for example, would use an Eb Major scale starting on C as its chord scale.

CHAPTER TWO
Minor Chord Scale Exercises
Part One: Scales and Exercises

C Minor 7th Scale
(C Dorian)

Exercise

F Minor 7th Scale
(F Dorian)

Exercise

B♭ Minor 7th Scale
(B♭ Dorian)

Exercise

38

E♭ Minor 7th Scale
(E♭ Dorian)

Exercise

EL96113

A♭ Minor 7th Scale
(A♭ Dorian)

Exercise

C♯ Minor 7th Scale
(C♯ Dorian)

Exercise

F♯ Minor 7th Scale
(F♯ Dorian)

Exercise

B Minor 7th Scale
(B Dorian)

Exercise

EL96113

42

E Minor 7th Scale
(E Dorian)

Exercise

A Minor 7th Scale
(A Dorian)

Exercise

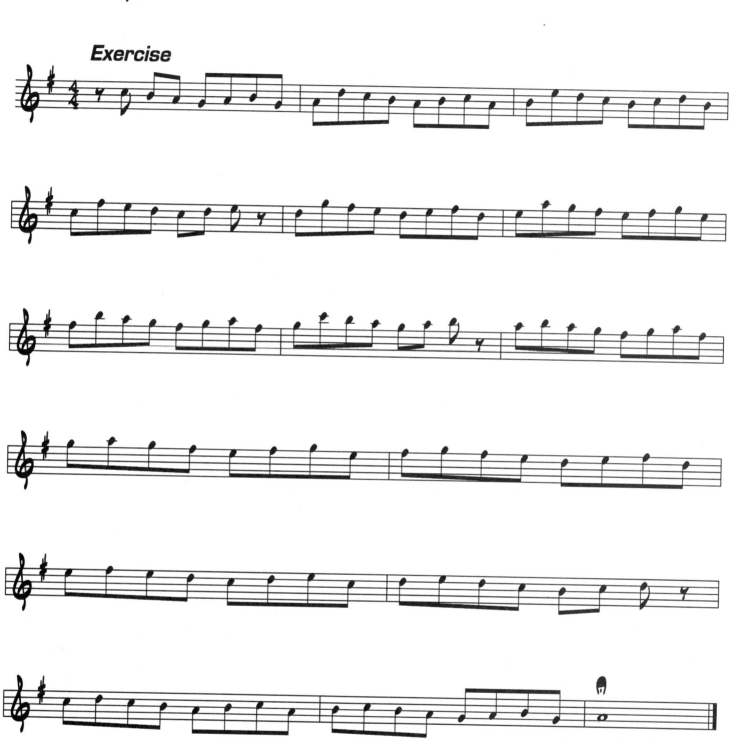

44

D Minor 7th Scale
(D Dorian)

Exercise

G Minor 7th Scale
(G Dorian)

Exercise

Part Two: Motif Exercises

1

Minor 2nd's

46

Major 2nd's

Minor 3rd's

48

2

Minor 2nd's

Major 2nd's

Major 2nd's

Minor 3rd's

Major 3rd's

Perfect 4th's

54

Major 7th's

Octaves

Part Three: "Finger Busters"

Part Four: Extended Motifs

Part Five: Ideas for Improvising

This section deals with a solo written over a minor blues progression and it incorporates both min.7th and Dom.7th chords. As before, play through the solo and see how the phrases fit into the chord changes above.

Throughout this solo, various types of minor scales are used. The one you choose depends on your melodic preference. Since we've covered the dorian minor scale, here are some ideas using other minor scales over the Min.7th chord.

Ex.3
D Natural Minor
Dm

Ex.4
G Harmonic Minor
Gm

* B♭ Melodic Minor

* In this context, the Melodic Minor scale is the same both ascending and descending.

B♭m

Quick Reference

CHORD SCALE   MINOR (including Dorian, Natural, Harmonic, & Melodic)

CHORD TYPE: Min. 7th
                          Min. 9th
                          Min. 11th
                          Min. 13th
                          *Min.(Maj7th)
                          **Dom. 7th(♭9)(♭13)
                          ***Dom. 7(alt)

*Use a Harmonic or Melodic Minor scale.

**Use Harmonic Minor scale starting on the 5th degree.
For example, for C7(♭9)(♭13) you could use an F Harmonic Minor scale starting on C.

***You can use the Melodic Minor scale a half-step above the root of the altered chord as discussed in Chapter 4.

CHAPTER THREE
UNALTERED DOMINANT
CHORD SCALE EXERCISES
Part One: Scales and Exercises

D Dominant 7th Scale

Exercise

E♭ Dominant 7th Scale

Exercise

70

E Dominant 7th Scale

Exercise

EL96113

71

F Dominant 7th Scale

Exercise

F# Dominant 7th Scale

Exercise

EL96113

G Dominant 7th Scale

Exercise

A♭ Dominant 7th Scale

Exercise

A Dominant 7th Scale

Exercise

74

B Dominant 7th Scale

Exercise

EL96113

Part Two: Motif Exercises

1

Minor 3rd's

Major 3rd's

Perfect 4th's

Tri-Tones

Perfect 5th's

Minor 6th's

Major 6th's

Major 2nd's

Minor 3rd's

Major 3rd's

3

Minor 2nd's

Major 2nd's

Minor 3rd's

Part Three: "Finger Busters"

Part Four: Extended Motifs

90

EL96113

Part Five: Ideas for Improvising

This section deals with a solo written over a set of "Blues" Changes. As you play through this solo, as in the last chapter, see how each phrase fits into the chord above. The strong parts of the chord (root, 3rd, and 5th) are used as pivot points and the scale and chromatic passing tones are used to help shape the melodies.

EL96113

#1. Note how this first phrase emphasizes the strong parts of each chord and uses scale and chromatic passing tones to shape the melody.

#2. On a Dom.7(sus4) chord the 4th replaces the 3rd in the chord voicing and becomes a strong sound in the chord. This phrase pivots on the note, "C" which is the 4th of the G7(sus4) chord.

The Dominant 7th scale (or the Mixolydian Mode) comes from the 5th degree of the Major scale. For example, the G Mixolydian scale has the same notes as the C Major scale. You can also think of the Mixolydian scale as a Major scale with a flatted 7th. If you relate this scale to its Major scale origin, it may make it easier to play.

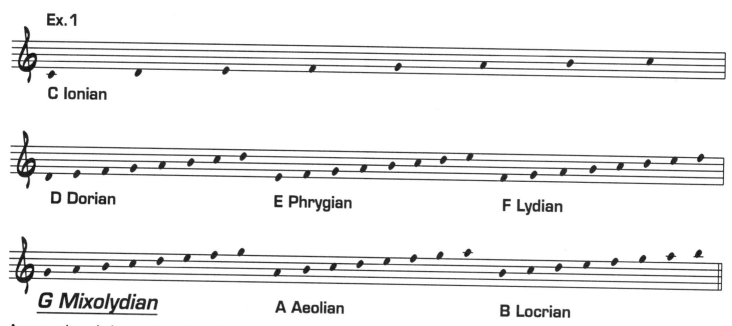

As you already know, "tensions" are notes that do not appear in the basic chord but sound good and give the chord different colors and characteristics. Here are the available tensions for Dominant 7th chords:

The scales used for playing over altered Dominant chords which may be notated as C7(alt), for example, are discussed in Chapters 4 and 5. Here are some other ideas for playing over Dom.7th chords:

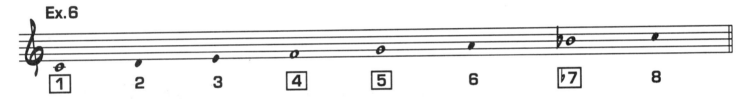

The Dom.7(sus4) chord shifts the emphasis of the phrase or melody from the 3rd to the 4th:

Here are some other ideas for playing over Dom.7(sus4) chords:

Ex. 9

One type of <u>Altered</u> Dominant chord scale that should be mentioned in this chapter is the Dom.7(#4) or the <u>Lydian Dominant</u> scale. Here is an example of a C7(#4) chord scale:

Ex. 10

Here are some other ideas for playing over Dom.7(#4) chords:

Ex. 11

Ex. 12

Ex. 13

Quick Reference

CHORD SCALE:	DOM. 7TH or MIXOLYD.	LYD. DOM.
CHORD TYPE	Dom. 7th	Dom. 7th(#11)
	Dom. 9th	Dom.7th(#11)(13)
	Dom.11th	*Maj7th(#5)
	Dom. 13th	
	Dom. 7th(sus4)	

*Use Lyd. Dom. scale a whole step above the root of the chord. For example, over C Maj7(#5) you can use the D Lyd. Dom. scale starting and ending on C. (It may be helpful to note that the D Lydian Dominant scale has the same notes as the A Melodic Minor Scale.)

CHAPTER FOUR
MELODIC MINOR CHORD SCALE EXERCISES

Part One: Scales and Exercises

C Melodic Minor

G Melodic Minor

Exercise

D Melodic Minor

Exercise

A Melodic Minor

Exercise

E Melodic Minor

Exercise

B Melodic Minor

Exercise

F♯ Melodic Minor

Exercise

C# Melodic Minor

Exercise

A♭ Melodic Minor

Exercise

E♭ Melodic Minor

Exercise

B♭ Melodic Minor

Exercise

F Melodic Minor

Exercise

Part Two: Motif Exercises

1

Minor 2nd's

108

Major 2nd's

Minor 3rd's

Major 3rd's

Major 2nd's

Minor 3rd's

Major 3rd's

Perfect 4th's

Tri-Tones

Perfect 5th's

Minor 6th's

Major 6th's

Minor 7th's

Major 7th's

Octaves

3

Minor 2nd's

116

Part Three: "Finger Busters"

Part Four: Extended Motifs

124

Part Five: Ideas For Improvising

This section deals with a solo written over several different types of chords that can all use the Melodic Minor scale as their chord scale. As you practice the solo study how the scale is being used and how it relates to the chord above.

#1. On min.7(♭5) chords, you can use the Melodic Minor scale a minor 3rd <u>above</u> the root of the chord. For example, on a C♯m7(♭5) chord, use E Melodic Minor starting and ending on C♯.

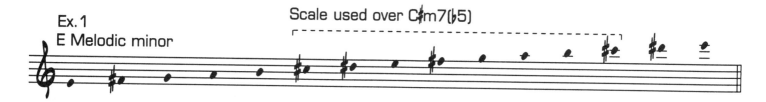

Ex. 1
E Melodic minor
Scale used over C♯m7(♭5)

#2. On altered chords (that include ♭13's in their voicings), you can use the Melodic Minor scale a half-step <u>above</u> the root of the chord. For example, on an F♯7(alt) use G Melodic Minor starting and ending on F♯.

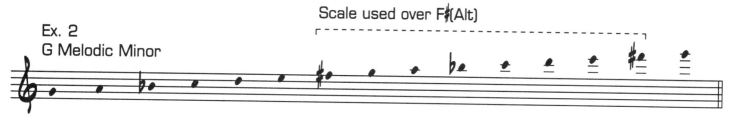

Ex. 2
G Melodic Minor
Scale used over F♯(Alt)

#3. On any minor triad or min.(Maj7) chords, you can use the Melodic Minor scale starting on the root of the chord. For example, on an Am or Am(Maj7), one scale you can use is A Melodic Minor.

#4. On a 13(♯11) chord or any Lydian Dominant chord, (C7(♯11) for example), you can use the Melodic Minor scale a 5th <u>above</u> the root of the chord. For example, on D13(♯11) use A Melodic Minor starting and ending on D.

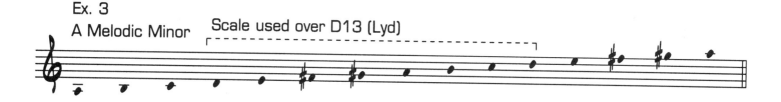

Ex. 3
A Melodic Minor
Scale used over D13 (Lyd)

#5. On Maj7(♯5) chords, you can use the Melodic Minor scale a minor 3rd below the root of the chord. For example, on F Maj7(♯5) use D Melodic Minor starting and ending on F.

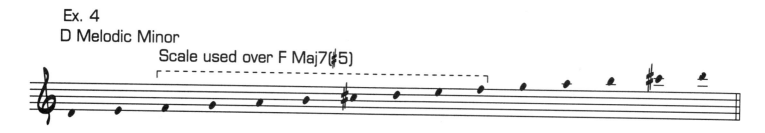

Ex. 4
D Melodic Minor
Scale used over F Maj7(♯5)

<u>*Quick Reference*</u>

<u>CHORD SCALE:</u>   <u>MELODIC MINOR</u>

<u>CHORD TYPE:</u>   Minor 7th
Minor 9th
Minor 11th
Minor 13th
Min.(Maj7th)
*Min.7(♭5)
**Dom.7(♭9)(♭13)
**Dom.7(♭9)(♯9)
**Dom.7(♭9)(♯11)
**Dom.7(♭9)(♯11)(♭13)
**Dom.7(♯9)(♯11)(♭13)
**Dom.7(♭9)(♯9)(♯11)(♭13)
**Dom.7(♯9)(♯11)(♭13)
***Maj7(♯5)

* For Min.7(♭5) chords, use the Melodic Minor scale a min. 3rd above the root of the chord.
  Ex. For Cm7(♭5), use E♭ Mel. Min. starting on C.

**For all of these Dom.7(alt) chords, use the Melodic Minor scale a half-step above the root of the
  chord (as long as the 13th is flat).
  Ex. For C7(alt), use D♭ Mel. Min. starting on C.

*** For Maj7(♯5) chords, use the Melodic Minor scale a minor 3rd below the root of the chord.
  Ex. For CMaj7(♯5), use A Mel. Min. starting on C.

CHAPTER FIVE
DIMINISHED CHORD SCALE EXERCISES

Part One: Scales and Exercises

C Diminished Scale

Exercise

C# Diminished Scale

Exercise

D Diminished Scale

Exercise

E♭ Diminished Scale

Exercise

E Diminished Scale

Exercise

F Diminished Scale

Exercise

F# Diminished Scale

Exercise

136

B♭ Diminished Scale

Exercise

B Diminished Scale

Exercise

Part Two: Motif Exercises

Minor 2nd's

Major 2nd's

Minor 3rd's

Major 3rd's

139

EL96113

2

Minor 2nd's

Major 2nd's

Minor 3rd's

Major 3rd's

142

EL96113

3

Minor 2nd's

144

Major 2nd's

Minor 3rd's

Part Three: "Finger Busters"

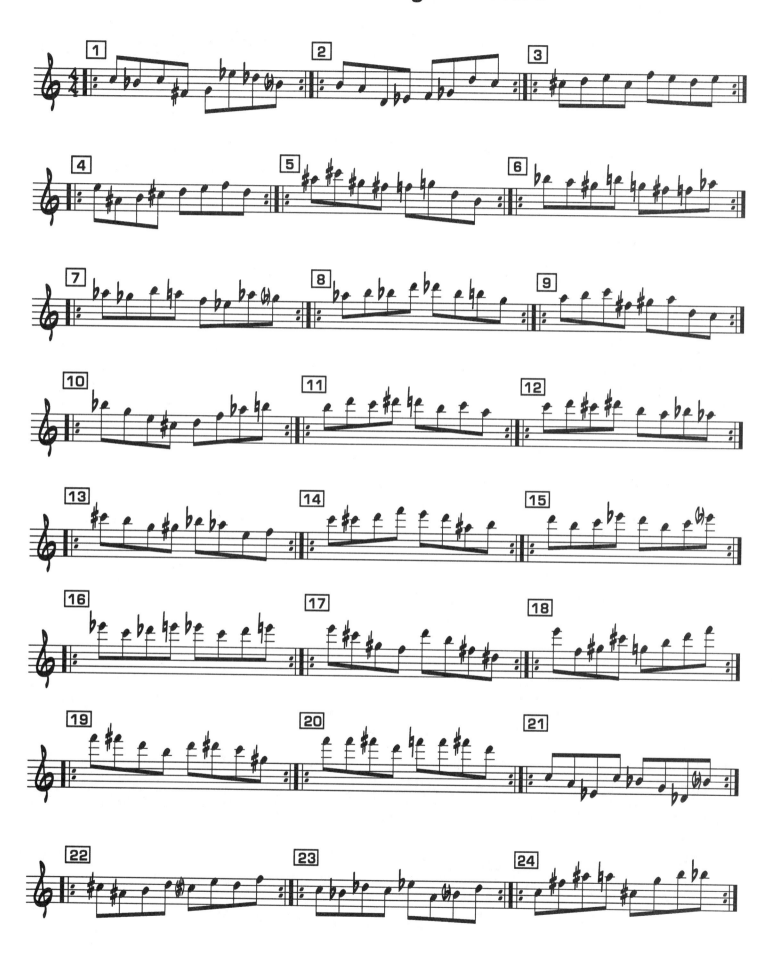

Part Four: Extended Motifs

Part Five: Ideas for Improvising

This section deals with a solo written over several different types of chords that can all use the Diminished scale as their chord scale. As you practice this, try to see which Diminished scale is being used and how it relates to the chord above.

#1. Any altered Dom. 7th chord with a natural 13th can use a Diminished scale as it's chord scale.

Ex. 1

#2. If a Dominant chord is altered in some way, (in this case with a ♭9th), and doesn't indicate a flat 13th or a natural 13th, you can you the Diminished scale.

#3. On Diminished chords, it usually sounds better to use the traditional whole step/half step Diminished scale.

#4. A Major triad with the minor 2nd in the base, (F♯/G), can use an F♯ Diminished chord.

CHAPTER SIX
PENTATONIC AND BLUES SCALE EXERCISES

Part One: Scales and Exercises

C Minor Pentatonic

Exercise

C Blues Scale

Exercise

C# Minor Pentatonic

Exercise

C# Blues Scale

Exercise

D Minor Pentatonic

Exercise

D Blues Scale

Exercise

162

Eb Minor Pentatonic

Exercise

Eb Blues scale

Exercise

164

EL96113

F# Minor Pentatonic

Exercise

F♯ Blues Scale

Exercise

G Minor Pentatonic

Exercise

G Blues Scale

Exercise

A♭ Minor Pentatonic

Exercise

A♭ Blues Scale

Exercise

A Minor Pentatonic

Exercise

B♭ Blues Scale

Exercise

171

EL96113

Part Two: Motif Exercises

1

Minor 2nd's

Major 2nd's

Minor 7th's

Major 7th's

Octaves

2

Minor 2nd's

Major 2nd's

Minor 3rd's

Major 3rd's

Perfect 4th's

Tri-Tones

Perfect 5th's

Minor 6th's

Major 6th's

Minor 7th's

Major 7th's

Octaves

3

Minor 2nd's

Major 2nd's

Minor 3rd's

Major 3rd's

Perfect 4th's

Part Three: "Finger Busters"

Part Four: Extended Motifs

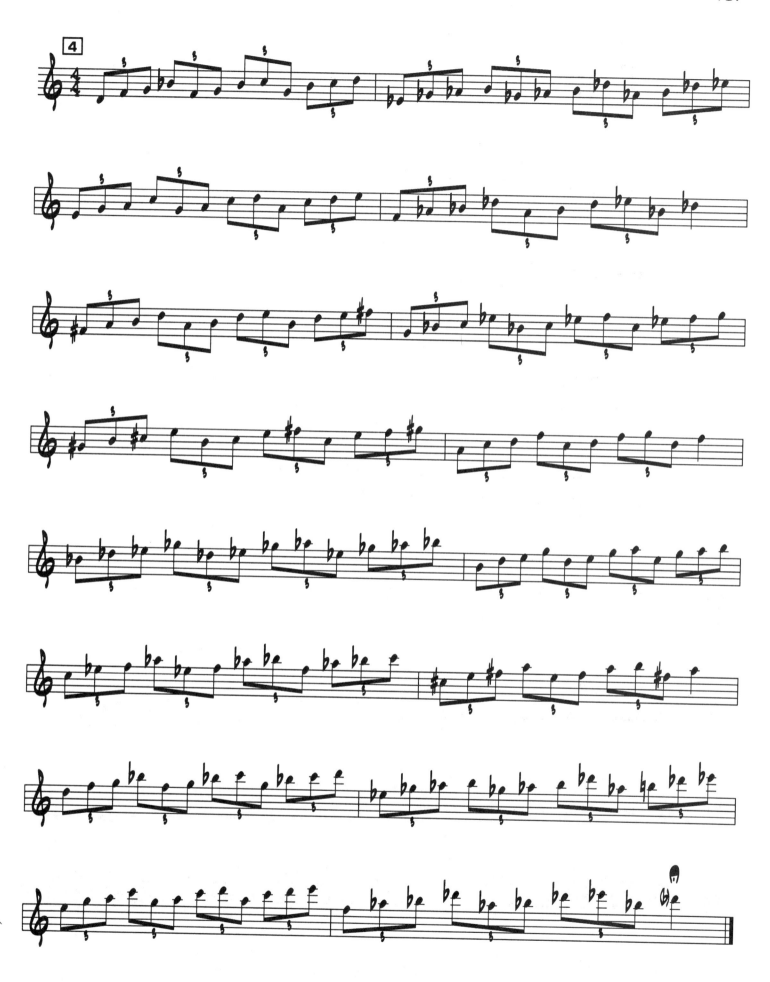

Part Five: Ideas for Improvising

This section deals with a written solo that shows some ideas for using Pentatonic and Blues scales over various types of chords. These are only a few examples of chords that these scales work over but, as you can see by the "Quick Reference" at the end of the chapter, there are many more.

190

#1. Here is an example of a Pentatonic and a Blues scale used over Dominant 7th chords.

#2. Pentatonic and Blues scales work great over Minor chords.

#3. On Major(sus) chords you can use the Major Pentatonic scale which starts and ends on the 2nd degree of the Minor Pentatonic scale and uses the same notes.

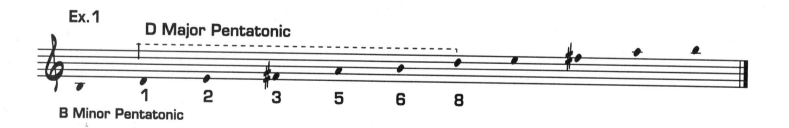

Quick Reference

CHORD SCALE:	MAJ. PENT.	MIN. PENT.	BLUES SCALE
CHORD TYPE:	All Maj6 chords All unalt. Doms. *Dom.7(♯5)(♯9)	All min. chords (including min. sus chords). **Maj7(♯11) *** All Dom.(sus) chords.	All min. chords. All alt. & unalt. Doms.

*Use Major pent. scale a minor 6th above the root of the chord. For example, on C7(♯5)(♯9), you can use the A♭ Major pent. scale.

** Use minor pent. a half step below the root of the chord. For example, on CMaj7(♯11), you can use the B minor pent. scale.

*** Use minor pent. a 4th below the root of the chord. For example, on C7(sus), you can use the G minor pent. scale.